Now You're Cooking!

Now You're Cooking!

Ten Short Stories with Recipes

Edited by Diane M. Lynch

BOOKS & MEDIA
Boston

Library of Congress Cataloging-in-Publication Data

Now you're cooking! : ten short stories with recipes / edited by Diane M. Lynch.
    v. cm.
  "Some stories in this collection first appeared in *My Friend, the Catholic magazine for kids*."
  Contents: Stirring up trouble / by Diana R. Jenkins -- Recipes for disaster / by Rosemarie Dicristo -- Pot lucky / by Renee Riede -- Aunt Lil's magic muffins / by Linda Vilcone -- A taste of the world / by Christine Venzon -- Am I skinny yet? / by Diana R. Jenkins -- Grading Gran / by Donna R. Gamache -- Unplugged for a week / by Christine Brauer Mueller -- Attack of the cousins! / by Diana R. Jenkins -- The breakfast battle / by Leanne K. Currie-Mcghee.
  ISBN 0-8198-5167-1 (pbk.)
  1. Children's stories, American. [1. Short stories. 2. Cookery--Fiction. 3. Christian life--Fiction.] I. Lynch, Diane M., date. II. Title: Now you're cooking!
  PZ5.N72 2009
  [Fic]--dc22

                                    2009007214

Introduction and recipes by Diane M. Lynch

Cover art by David Leonard

Design by Mary Joseph Peterson, FSP

Some stories in this collection first appeared in *My Friend: The Catholic Magazine for Kids*.

Published by Pauline Books & Media, 50 Saint Pauls Avenue, Boston, MA 02130-3491

Printed in the U.S.A.

www.pauline.org

Pauline Books & Media is the publishing house of the Daughters of St. Paul, an international congregation of women religious serving the Church with the communications media.

1 2 3 4 5 6 7 8 9   13 12 11 10 09

Contents

Welcome	**6**
Read This Section Before You Cook	**7**
Mealtime Prayers	**11**
Stirring Up Trouble By Diana R. Jenkins	**13**
Recipes for Disaster By Rosemarie DiCristo	**22**
Pot Lucky By Renee Riede	**34**
Aunt Lil's Magic Muffins By Linda Vilcone	**44**
A Taste of the World By Christine Venzon	**52**
Am I Skinny Yet? By Diana R. Jenkins	**62**
Grading Gran By Donna R. Gamache	**74**
Unplugged for a Week By Christine Brauer Mueller	**86**
Attack of the Cousins! By Diana R. Jenkins	**97**
The Breakfast Battle By Leanne K. Currie-McGhee	**108**
Recipe Index	**121**

Welcome

Welcome to *Now You're Cooking!*

Have you ever heard the saying, "You are what you eat"?

Well, of course, we can't take that too literally (although, you must admit, it would be kind of hilarious). What *is* true, though, is that food is a lot more than just what keeps us alive. All over the world, thanking God for food and enjoying a meal with friends and family are a big part of celebrations, holidays, and daily life.

In each of these fun short stories, food or cooking plays a role of some kind. Every story is followed by one or two recipes for some of the foods that appeared. Enjoy reading the stories, and try the recipes, too! Be sure to read the next section before you begin to cook; it contains important cooking and safety tips. And before you eat, it's always great to take a moment to say "thank you" to God.

Happy reading—and cooking!

Read This Section Before You Cook

Basic Cooking Tips

1. Always read each recipe thoroughly before you begin cooking. Make sure you understand each step. If something isn't clear, check with an adult.

2. Gather the ingredients you'll need before you start. Measure them carefully. Use a dry measuring cup for dry ingredients and a liquid measuring cup for wet ones. To measure dry ingredients, spoon them into a heap in the measuring cup. Level off the top with the flat side of a knife. You can use the same technique for measuring dry ingredients in measuring spoons.

3. When a recipe calls for butter, you can always substitute margarine (in stick form) instead. When a recipe says to grease a pan, you can either spray it with cooking spray or rub it with a thin film of butter or margarine. If the recipe says to butter and flour a pan, first spray or rub it, then sprinkle flour inside and tilt the pan in different directions, tapping

it to be sure the bottom and sides of the pan get a thin coating of flour. When you're through, you can discard any extra flour. (Tip: Do this over the sink, so you won't have a messy countertop if you spill.)

4. To peel garlic, first separate the clove from the head of garlic. Place the flat part of a metal spatula over the clove, and use your fist to smash down on it. Smashing the clove will make the papery skin easy to pull off with your fingers. You can then carefully chop the garlic as directed.

4. Always wash your hands before cooking. If your hair gets in the way, tie it back or pin it.

5. Wearing an apron is a good idea—it will protect your clothes from spills and smudges.

6. Part of cooking is leaving the kitchen neat. Remember to clean up when you're done!

Keep It Safe!

Cooking is lots of fun, but you have to use common sense when you're doing it.

1. Check with an adult before you begin to cook.

2. Always use oven mitts or potholders when handling hot pans or lifting hot lids. Ask an adult for help if necessary.

3. Hot pans could harm a countertop or table. Instead, set them on a heatproof trivet, rack, or board.

4. Always turn pot handles away from the front of the stove, away from the heat. (That way, pots are less likely to tip over.)

5. Be very careful with knives. Dry your hands before you use them (wet hands can cause knives to slip). Ask an adult for help when necessary.

6. Ask an adult for permission to use electrical equipment like mixers or blenders, and be sure to follow directions when using them. Keep fingers, spoons, and other utensils out of machinery when it is running!

6. Make sure you turn off the stove or oven when you're finished.

Keep It Clean!

1. Wash your hands thoroughly before you begin cooking. Always wash them again after handling raw meat.

2. Wash all raw fruits and vegetables under running water before preparing them.

3. Use a separate cutting board for meats and for fruits

or vegetables. Don't put cooked food and raw food on the same plate.

4. Keep your cooking area clean! Have paper towels or a dishcloth handy to wipe up spills.

5. Always keep meat in the refrigerator until you're ready to use it.

6. Close kitchen drawers before you start cooking. That way, spills won't end up inside them!

How Easy Is This Recipe?

Next to each recipe, you'll see one, two, or three spoons. Here's what they mean:

 Quick & Easy

 A Little More Complicated

 Most Challenging

Mealtime Prayers

Prayer before Meals

Bless us, O Lord,
and these your gifts
which we are about to receive from your bounty,
through Christ our Lord. Amen.

Prayer after Meals

We give you thanks
for all your benefits,
O loving God,
you who live and reign
forever. Amen.

Stirring Up Trouble

By Diana R. Jenkins

When Mrs. Taylor partnered me with Jen, I felt pretty hopeful. Some kids goof around in activity classes like home ec, but Jen seemed like a hard worker. I take my grades seriously, and I needed a partner with the right attitude.

"I want an A in this class," I told her when we met at our cooking station. "Don't you?"

"Sure, David," said Jen. "But—"

"Good. Let's get busy." I looked at our recipe card. "Hmmm . . . broccoli salad. You start the dressing, and I'll cut up broccoli."

I was glad to see that Jen measured carefully. I hadn't cooked much, but wasn't a recipe just a bunch of directions? If we followed the steps exactly, we'd make a perfect dish—and a perfect grade!

After the broccoli was ready, Jen added chopped onion to the bowl and poured on the dressing. Then I stirred everything together. We each tried some, and the salad was really tasty!

"It's good," said Jen, "but it needs something." She searched in the cupboard, took out a box, and dumped whatever was in it into our salad.

"Ew!" She was stirring raisins into our perfect dish! "That's not in the recipe!"

"But I bet it will be good."

"Raisins and broccoli? I don't think so!"

I was going to fish the raisins out, but Mrs. Taylor came along to taste our work. "Interesting," she said. Then she marked her grade book and moved to the next station.

"She's probably giving us an F," I hissed at Jen. "You shouldn't have messed with the recipe."

"Oh, relax," she said. "It's fun to experiment when you're cooking."

We had six weeks until we switched to Industrial Technology—I couldn't let Jen experiment with my grade all that time! "Just stick to the recipes from now on. Okay?"

"Whatever," she said.

I didn't eat any of our ruined salad, but other kids tried it and said it was good. Just to be nice, I guess.

The next time we cooked, Mrs. Taylor gave us a recipe for sugar cookies. Jen and I quickly measured and combined the ingredients. Then she said, "This dough looks boring."

I didn't want her to go raisin-crazy again. "It's fine! We followed the recipe exactly." I started spooning some dough onto a cookie sheet.

"Wait!" she cried. "Should the pan be greased?"

I checked the recipe card. "It doesn't really say." Could a detail like that ruin our cookies? "I'd better ask Mrs. Taylor."

I had to follow the teacher around awhile until I could ask my question. When I returned to our station, the cookies were already baking!

"I figured if we were supposed to grease the pan the recipe would say so," said Jen.

That's what Mrs. Taylor told me, too, but Jen didn't know that! "What if you were wrong?" I demanded.

She rolled her eyes. "I guess that was a risk I was willing to take."

The cookies came out suspiciously lumpy. I turned to Jen. "Hey . . ."

"Interesting!" Mrs. Taylor had appeared at my elbow. She tried a cookie and said, "Very interesting." She wrote in her grade book and moved on.

"What are those lumps?" I asked when the teacher was out of earshot.

Jen grinned. "Potato chips! I had some in my pack. I just crunched—"

"Are you trying to make us flunk?" I yelled. "We. Have. To. Follow. The. Recipes!"

"Well, what fun is that?" said Jen.

While other kids snarfed our freaky cookies, I cleaned the counter and thought about my situation. Jen was causing a lot of trouble, but complaining to Mrs. Taylor might just stir up more problems for me. What if it looked like I wasn't cooperating? I decided I'd just have to watch Jen closely.

But no matter how I tried, I couldn't keep her from messing up every recipe. She wrecked our baked beans with cranberry sauce—I thought she was pouring in another can of beans! While I looked for a pan, she added sauerkraut to our brownie batter. And she tossed some black pepper into our chocolate cookie dough before I could even react!

"You're ruining everything!" I cried as she stirred in the pepper.

"Relax, David," she said. "Cooking is supposed to be—"

"Fun! I know! And maybe it would be, if I had a partner who wasn't an idiot!"

Jen threw down her wooden spoon and stomped out, leaving me to make and bake a million balls of dough by myself. Then she came back just in time to hear Mrs. Taylor call our project "interesting" and to join the other kids in gobbling everything up. Like usual! I didn't touch the stuff, of course.

Our next project was the last of the grading period, and I was determined to make it perfect. We had to impress Mrs. Taylor and save our grades!

But Jen just stood there, pouting, while I made our chicken vegetable soup. It wasn't hard to do, but . . . well . . . the whole thing was boring without a partner.

As we waited for the soup to boil, I noticed that Jen's eyes looked sad. I must have really hurt her feelings! Okay, she had destroyed my grade, but not on purpose. She just wanted us to have a good time. Too bad she got stuck with a partner who didn't really enjoy fun!

Mrs. Taylor came along and peered into the pot. "I'll bet that's delicious. You two are the most creative cooks I've ever had!"

After Mrs. Taylor walked away, I couldn't even look at Jen. She hadn't ruined our grades at all! Could I have cooked up a bigger mess? And could I fix things?

That's when I got an idea. I ran to the pantry and grabbed the first jar I saw. Back at our station, I wrestled the lid off the jar and poured half its contents into the pot.

"Salsa?" said Jen. "That's not in the recipe!"

I picked up the spoon and blended the salsa into the soup. "There's nothing wrong with stirring things up when you're cooking." We both laughed and then I said, "I'm sorry, okay?"

"Okay," she said. "Hey, are there any tortilla chips around here?"

"For the soup?" I cried. Then I nodded and said, "Interesting!"

For once, I actually tried what we'd cooked. Our soup was delicious! Too bad I hadn't been able to relax enough to enjoy our other dishes. But when we switch to Industrial Technology, I'm planning to have a good time. Who knows? Maybe I'll get Jen as my partner again. Now that would be a recipe for fun!

Creative Chicken Salsa Soup

Here's the recipe that earned David and Jen the top grade in their home ec class!

Serves 4

- 2 cans low-sodium chicken broth (14.5 ounces each)

- 1 cup chopped cooked chicken

- 1 teaspoon chili powder (add more if you like it spicier—but be sure to taste first!)

- 1 can whole-kernel corn, drained (11 ounces)

- 1 medium green pepper, chopped

- 1 cup chunky-style salsa (you can choose mild, medium, or hot)

- 3 cups broken tortilla chips (put them in a plastic bag and *lightly* crush with a rolling pin. (Don't crush too heavily, or you'll end up with tortilla crumbs!)

- 1/4 cup shredded Monterey Jack or cheddar cheese

1. Put the chicken broth, chicken, chili powder, corn, and green pepper into a pot.

2. Bring to a boil and simmer on low for 8 minutes.

3. Stir in the salsa and heat through.

4. Ladle into bowls, top with chips, and sprinkle with the cheese.

Recipes for Disaster

Or, The Cookies that (Almost) Crushed Cliveden, Texas

By Rosemarie DiCristo

Never Perfect

I, Rachelle Miranda Donnelly, have always wanted to excel at things. Okay, who wouldn't? But I've got a special reason. My sister, Allison Elizabeth Donnelly, excels at everything. I, on the other hand, have a tendency to mess things up, especially cooking—the one thing I really love doing.

Example? The chocolate cake I made for Allison's middle school graduation sank in the middle like a deflated balloon. I had no idea the baking powder I accidentally left out was so important.

Example? The brownies I made to celebrate her soccer championship had the delicate texture of . . . bricks. I guess how long you leave them in the oven really does matter.

Conclusion? I desperately needed to start doing things right.

The Belated Birthday Dinner

On January 14, Dad celebrated his fortieth birthday. I was scheduled to cook his birthday feast.

"Make sure you make something Italian," was his only request. Dad l-o-v-e-s Italian food.

The lasagna should've been delicious. Chockfull of meatballs and sausage. Loaded with mozzarella and ricotta. Drenched in an absolutely super tomato sauce. What went wrong, you ask?

Somehow I didn't set the oven temperature right. Just so you know, baking lasagna at 125° F for one hour doesn't give you quite the same result as baking it at 325° F.

Have you ever had warmish, nearly-raw lasagna? Not good.

Allison-the-perfect-sister tried to be positive. "Anyone can read things wrong, Rae. I've done it myself."

I sighed, then baked the lasagna properly. Dinner was a little late. An unforgivable failure? Maybe not. But when your sister's perfect . . . you wanna be good at things, too, right? Right.

That's what led me to:

The Mexican Hockey Horror

Allison's team—the Cliveden Cougars—won this year's playoffs. And last year's. And two years ago, too. To show I was happy for her, I invited her and the rest of the Cougars to lunch.

The Olé Chicken Casserole I made for the Cougars included chicken, canned soup, salsa, broth, and taco chips. Well, it should have been okay. Unfortunately, the recipe was on the left-hand page, and partway through putting it together, I had a brain cramp and started reading the directions from the recipe on the right-hand page. Hey, it could happen to anyone, right? But the ingredient list on the right-hand page happened to end with two teaspoons of salt. And since I was quadrupling the recipe, that turned out to be one salty Mexican casserole.

"It's . . . different," Karly Marvin said.

"It's . . . interesting," Denise Brodsky said.

"It's dehydrating me," Sharly Simonelli said. (She's team goalie and way outspoken.)

Allison said brightly, "I think it's tasty."

Did I mention that in addition to being pretty, athletic, and smart, Allison won Miss Congeniality last year?

Bottom line—another success for Allison. Another failure for me. Which led to:

Angry Moments

"You promised to do *what* for the Cliveden Community Center?" Allison yelped.

"The absolute shock in your voice is just slightly insulting," I said.

"Seriously," Allison said. "You'll bake? Twelve dozen cookies? For their awards banquet?"

I narrowed my eyes. Allison sounded like she was one second away from flopping to the floor in a dead faint. "Okay," I said. "Those meals I destroyed might've been a little too ambitious, but cookies are a snap."

Allison's eyebrows went all furrowed, like they do when she's thinking something she doesn't want to say. "Why are you doing this, Rae?"

"Well, of course I want to help out!"

Allison still looked mega-serious. "So your reasons have nothing to do with Channel Five filming the banquet? Or me getting that award from the Cliveden Senior Citizens Club?"

"No," I said. "I'm trying to do something nice."

"Rae," she said softly, "you don't have to be perfect."

"No," I shot back. "You're perfect enough for both of us."

Allison's face went dull red. "You've always been jealous of me. Of everything I do."

My face went blazing-red-hot. "That's not true!"

"No? Even that chicken stuff you made for our hockey championship was more about you showing off than you being happy for me."

"That's not true!" I said again. "I was thrilled you won that stupid championship." Oops. Didn't mean to say that. "Sorry."

Allison just stared at me. She wasn't angry. She looked like she understood.

Understood? Perfect Allison? Impossible!

I said, "If I could do just one thing perfectly ..."

"Did you ever think," Allison said, "the reason I do five things perfectly is because I'm afraid of failing? You're okay with it. When you make mistakes, you laugh. But me . . . !"

"You're still perfect," I said.

She shook her head. "No one's perfect. Trying hard is what matters. And being nice."

"You're nice, too," I said sourly.

"So are you. You're a good person."

"But I want to be good *at things*," I explained.

Those Crushing Cookies

I'll make this one short and sweet. The instructions read "Place teaspoon-sized balls of dough 2 inches apart," but I thought it would save time to make the spice cookies bigger and crowd them together a little. Well, maybe more than a little. After all, they were industrial-sized pans, right?

Well, who knew they'd all merge together and turn into four pans of one gigantic cookie each? Humongous. Massive. Each one threatened to take over the pan, the oven, the community center, and the town of Cliveden, Texas, population 9,078, incorporated 1881.

I burst into tears. I also prayed.

"Please, God, maybe I was too focused on perfection, but in two hours, twenty-five award winners and their families will be here expecting cookies with their beef stew. Don't punish them because I was wrong."

Silence . . .

I peered through the oven window. The mutant cookies continued to puff and expand, threatening to flow over the sides of the pan and into the burner.

I prayed harder. "Okay, trying to be perfect just to top my sister is wrong." I raised my voice. "I'll change! If you just save these cookies, I'll never try to be perfect again!"

No luck; I took the pans out of the oven and put them on racks to cool. I had to send out something, so I cut them into squares, piled them on plates, and hoped for the best.

Shockingly, every crumb got devoured.

Afterward, Mayor Hooper told me, "Your hermits were delicious!"

"Hermits? They weren't exactly hermits—"

Mayor Hooper interrupted. "They were great! What else do you bake?"

Great? My mind started whirling. "Well, all kinds of cookies, really . . ."

The mayor requested eight dozen of the hermits for his son's Boy Scout troop. Allison's helping me make them. That's okay, because she's also helping me keep that promise about not being so focused on being perfect. And maybe it's kind of a good idea to have someone double-checking my recipe-reading skills.

Plus I'm beginning to realize what a fantabulous sister she really is. Not once has she mentioned how, the last time I melted chocolate, I accidentally left it in the microwave for so long it incinerated.

Anyway, no way could I possibly make that kind of mistake again.

Could I?

Hermits (that Almost Crushed Cliveden)

After Rachelle's first almost-disastrous attempt at these cookies, she changed the recipe so she could make them in a baking pan—instead of watching them overflow the edges of her cookie sheets!

Makes 24 cookie bars

1 3/4 cups all-purpose flour

1/2 teaspoon baking soda

1/2 teaspoon salt

1 teaspoon cinnamon

1/2 teaspoon nutmeg

1/4 teaspoon ground cloves

1/2 cup butter (1 stick), softened

2/3 cup packed dark brown sugar (to measure, tamp it down with a spoon)

1 large egg

1/4 cup molasses

1 cup raisins

1/2 cup chopped walnuts (you can leave these out if you don't like nuts)

1. Preheat oven to 350° F.

2. Butter and flour a 13 x 9-inch baking pan.

3. In a medium-size bowl, stir together flour, baking soda, salt, cinnamon, nutmeg, and cloves.

4. In another bowl, use an electric mixer to beat the butter and brown sugar until they are fluffy, or beat by hand with a wooden spoon (it will take about 5 minutes).

5. Add the egg and the molasses, and beat well.

6. Add the flour mixture, about 1/2 cup at a time, mixing each time until the dry ingredients are combined (batter will be stiff).

7. Stir in the raisins and walnuts.

8. Spread the mixture evenly in the baking pan. (Tip: for easy spreading, slip your hand inside a plastic sandwich bag, then use it to lightly press down the batter so it's evenly distributed.)

9. Bake for 15 to 20 minutes. Check for doneness by inserting a toothpick in the center; when the toothpick comes out dry, the hermits are done. The top should be browned.

10. Let the pan cool completely on a rack.

11. Cut into 24 bars. Store in an airtight container.

Pot Lucky

By Renee Riede

"Watch your step, Mrs. Tran!" Grandpa says, holding the door open for his neighbor as she tiptoes into the lobby of their big brick apartment building.

Mrs. Tran smiles and nods, but she doesn't say a word to Grandpa or me. Not even when we ride the elevator together all the way to the seventh floor, which is where all three of us get off.

"Can Mrs. Tran talk?" I ask, as Grandpa sets up the checkerboard on his kitchen table.

"Of course she can, Frankie," Grandpa chuckles, letting me have the red checkers, the way he always does, since red is my favorite color.

"Then why doesn't she ever say anything?"

"I think that she's afraid she might make a mistake," Grandpa says. "Mrs. Tran's first language is Vietnamese. She's still learning to speak English."

"Well, if she's so afraid to speak English, maybe she shouldn't have come here."

"Whoa, Frankie!" Grandpa frowns as I jump two of his black checkers.

"Poor sport," I laugh.

"Oh, I don't care a lick about those old checkers you jumped," Grandpa says.

"You don't?" I'm starting to feel a little bit mixed up because Grandpa looks pretty grumpy.

"Nope, but what you just said sure bothers me! Frankie, did I ever tell you who taught me to play checkers when I was right around your age?" Grandpa says, rocking back in his chair.

"I don't think so," I say, shaking my head. "Did that person make you mad or something?"

"Oh, no. Not at all," Grandpa says. "It's just that Mrs. Tran reminds me of him."

"She does? Was he from Vietnam?"

"No, he was from Italy," Grandpa says.

"Then why does Mrs. Tran remind you of him?"

"Because he was pretty nervous about speaking English, too." A smile is tugging at the corners of Grandpa's mouth, as if just thinking about that guy from Italy is enough to cheer him up.

"Well, who was he? Aren't you going to tell me? Come on, Grandpa. Puh-leease."

"Do you really, reeeeally, reeeeeeeeeally want to know?" Grandpa teases.

"Graaaaaandpaaaaaaaa," I whine.

"That man was none other than your great-great grandpa, Francesco Brunetti, from Pisa, Italia," Grandpa grins.

"My great-great grandpa was afraid to speak English?"

"Maybe afraid is the wrong word," Grandpa says. "Shy is probably the word I'm looking for. He was a little bit shy about speaking English."

"Gosh," I say, thinking about Ernesto and Sharam and Sofia, who all went to day camp with me. They all moved here from somewhere else, too. "I guess there are lots of people like my great-great grandpa living here in the USA."

"There certainly are," Grandpa agrees. "Why, even this apartment building is a regular old melting pot."

"You can say that again, Grandpa! This place is so hot in the summer, it's more like a boiling pot."

"Frankie," Grandpa explains, "what I mean is it's a melting pot because people from all over the world live here. We're all mixed up together in a great, big, amazingly, fabulous . . . um . . . uh . . . do you hear that, Frankie?"

"I sure do," I nod. Someone is knocking softly on the door of Grandpa's apartment.

"Let's see who it is," Grandpa says, and I jump up to open the door.

It's Grandpa's neighbor, Mrs. Tran, and she's holding a plate piled with little wrapped-up white bundles. In the middle of the plate, there's a bowl of some kind of sauce.

"Spring rolls!" Grandpa claps.

"For you and Grandson," Mrs. Tran whispers, handing the plate to Grandpa.

"Bless your heart, Mrs. Tran," Grandpa declares. "I thought we were going to be stuck with peanut butter for lunch. Won't you please come in?"

"For minute," Mrs. Tran says with a bow. "I need do more cooking, for what is called again please?"

"It's called a potluck, Mrs. Tran," Grandpa says. "And all the people in the building will be bringing lots of great things to the potluck for everyone to eat. Although," he adds, "I can't imagine that anyone will be bringing anything more delicious than your spring rolls."

"Oh, yes?" Mrs. Tran smiles, and her face is almost as red as my checkers. She looks very, very happy.

"You try, Grandson," Mrs. Tran says, nodding at the plate of spring rolls in my Grandpa's hands.

I grab a spring roll, dip it in the little bowl of sauce, and take a bite. "Wow!" I grin. "I can't believe it. These taste even better than they look!" I am *not* kidding.

"Okay, Grandson," Mrs. Tran smiles. "I bring more just for you to pot lucky."

"Pot lucky," Grandpa chuckles. "I couldn't have said it any better, Mrs. Tran."

"Okay," Mrs. Tran says, and she's still smiling and bowing as she backs out of Grandpa's apartment. "Okay!"

"What do you say we have some spring rolls while we finish that checkers match, Frankie?" Grandpa winks.

"Sounds great," I reply. "Let's do it."

On the day of the potluck, the picnic tables in the courtyard of the big brick apartment building are crowded with all kinds of amazing food, including Grandpa's cannelloni, Mrs. Poisson's crêpes, Mr. Garcia's tamales, Mrs. Tran's spring rolls, and an apple pie that I made with my mom.

"Grandson!" Mrs. Tran calls, waving me over to where she is sitting. "You come pot lucky!"

"Of course, Mrs. Tran," I say. "Actually, I feel pretty lucky that I was invited."

"All lucky here," Mrs. Tran smiles, looking around at all the people who are in the courtyard. "Lucky. Lucky. Lucky!"

"You said it, Mrs. Tran," I grin back.

And you know what? That's exactly how I feel to be part of this. Lucky, lucky, lucky!

Mrs. Tran's Vietnamese Spring Rolls

Eating these spring rolls really opened Frankie's eyes to how foods from different cultures have influenced the way Americans eat.

Rice paper wrappers (which come in a flat, round packages), rice noodles, and hoisin sauce are available in the Asian foods section of most grocery stores. Instead of chicken, you can use chopped cooked shrimp. You can also experiment with other vegetables for more variations.

Makes 8 rolls

8 round rice paper wrappers

2 ounces very thin dried rice noodles

1 cup cooked chicken, cut into thin strips

1 cup carrots (grated or cut in slivers)

1 cup cucumbers (peeled and grated or cut in slivers)

1/2 cup fresh bean sprouts

1/4 cup fresh mint leaves

1/4 cup fresh cilantro or parsley leaves

Dipping sauce (see recipes below)

1. Cook the noodles according to the package directions. Then drain them, rinse in cold water, and drain again.

2. Line up the cooked noodles, chicken, and vegetables, with each ingredient in its own bowl. This will let you put together your rolls in an efficient assembly-line operation!

3. Dip one piece of rice paper into a bowl of very hot water for 15 to 20 seconds to soften it. Take it out and lay it flat on a clean countertop. Then flip it over (this will help it to lie flatter).

4. Put a thin bundle of noodles (about as wide as your little finger) close to one edge of the wrapper. Roll that side of the wrapper over the noodles.

5. Put a bundle of chicken next to the noodles and roll the wrapper over that.

6. Do the same for the carrots, then the cucumber, then the bean sprouts. Sprinkle on two or three leaves of the mint and the cilantro or parsley.

7. Then fold the ends of the wrapper in, and fold the remaining side over to finish the roll.

8. Set on a plate, seam side down. (Keep the rolls separated so they don't stick together.)

9. If you're not eating the rolls right away, store them in the refrigerator, covered with a damp paper towel to keep them moist.

Peanut dipping sauce is Frankie's favorite, but Grandpa prefers soy-type sauce. Try them both to see which you like better! (Remember to check with your parents before cooking with peanut butter, since some kids are allergic to it.)

Frankie's Dipping Sauce

1/4 cup smooth peanut butter

1/4 cup hoisin sauce

1 tablespoon hot water

1 tablespoon low-sodium soy sauce

Whisk all ingredients together. If the sauce is too thick, add a little more hot water. Serve on the side.

Grandpa's Dipping Sauce

1 tablespoon unseasoned rice vinegar

1 tablespoon toasted sesame oil

1/2 cup low-sodium soy sauce

Stir vinegar, oil, and soy sauce together and serve on the side.

Aunt Lil's Magic Muffins

By Linda Vilcone

The morning after Aunt Lil arrived, I walked into the kitchen just in time to see her pulling a bunch of black bananas—ick!—out of our trash can.

"What are you doing?" I asked.

"Well, it seems a shame to waste these good bananas," Aunt Lil said.

"But that's the point—they aren't good bananas! That's why they're in the garbage."

"Let's see what happens if I put a magic spell on them," Aunt Lil said in a conspiratorial whisper as she wiggled her right index finger at the bananas. She seemed serious. Was she a lunatic or what?

Mom was excited about Aunt Lil's visit. We hadn't seen her for ten years because Aunt Lil had moved to Ireland when I was two. Now she was back living in the United States and visiting us for Thanksgiving. All my life she'd been sending cards for Christmas and birthdays, but for me it was like meeting her for the first time.

I thought maybe she'd look like my mom, who's her sister. But when she arrived last night, I couldn't believe that she was even related to us! Everyone else in Mom's family is tall and thin, with red hair and freckles. Aunt Lil is short and round, with brown hair and not a freckle in sight.

And what was with this pulling black bananas out of the kitchen trash and putting "spells" on them? Maybe Aunt Lil had actually gone over the edge—and really was crazy!

"Brittany, help!" Aunt Lil yelled, about an hour later. She sounded frantic! Did she start a fire in the kitchen or fall down? I raced into the kitchen, expecting to find a major catastrophe. Instead, Aunt Lil was calmly sitting at the table, drinking a cup of coffee.

"What's wrong, Aunt Lil?"

"Brittany, I need your help. Please sample one of these muffins and tell me if they're okay to keep, or if I should just throw them in the trash," she said with a serious look on her face. For the first time, I noticed the great smell in the kitchen. Then I saw the golden brown muffins sitting on cooling racks. I also noticed that those nasty bananas had disappeared from the counter.

"Where'd we get those muffins?"

"Well, after I put that spell on those bananas, I mashed them up and added some stuff," she said. "You taste them, and if they aren't any good we'll just throw them away."

I felt uneasy about those ancient black bananas. And what "stuff" did she add? Was Aunt Lil so nutty she might accidentally poison me?

"Will they make me sick?" I asked, still not so sure about the bananas.

"No, of course not!" Then, as if she was reading my mind, she added, "It's absolutely okay—I promise."

I put one on a plate and tentatively took a small bite, expecting it to taste, well, yucky. "Chocolate chips!" I said. The muffin melted in my mouth. It was delicious!

"If you throw these away, you really are crazy," I said, before taking another, larger bite. "These are the best muffins ever!"

"I guess my magic spell worked after all," Aunt Lil said. Then she started to laugh. Her laugh was infectious. I started giggling, too. In a few minutes we were both laughing so hard, tears were running down our cheeks and we were gasping for air.

All week Aunt Lil told me all kinds of stories about my mom and my grandparents. She put her fake spells on all of us and I watched her whole body shake like jelly when she laughed, which was often. Usually we'd all end up giggling together, unable to stop. She loves to cook, and I helped her make all kinds of great food like lasagna, homemade chicken noodle soup, and lots of cookies. We wrote down all of the recipes so I can make them after she goes home.

Being around Aunt Lil, I found out that it's okay to act silly, giggle, and play make-believe, even when you're practically a teenager—like me. The week flew by, and I was pretty sad when it came time for her to go home.

After I hugged her goodbye, I stood back and wiggled my index finger at her.

"Now who's magic?" I cried. "This time I'm putting a spell on you . . . to come back soon!"

Aunt Lil's Magic Muffins

Aunt Lil made these with chocolate chips, but you can substitute 1 cup of raisins, dried cranberries, or nuts. Mix and match if you prefer!

Makes about 12 muffins

  1/2 cup butter (1 stick), softened

  1 cup sugar

  2 eggs

  1 teaspoon vanilla extract

  2 cups all-purpose flour

  2 teaspoons baking powder

  1/2 teaspoon salt

  3 very ripe bananas (the blacker, the better!)

  1/2 cup milk

  1 cup chocolate chips

Topping

  3 tablespoons sugar

  1/4 teaspoon cinnamon

1. Preheat oven to 350° F.

2. Spray the cups of your muffin pan with cooking spray, or use muffin liners.

3. Put softened butter and sugar in a large mixing bowl and beat until light and fluffy, either with an electric beater or with a wooden spoon.

4. Add eggs, one at a time, blending well after adding each one.

5. Beat in vanilla.

6. Mix together flour, baking powder, and salt in a medium bowl. Set aside.

7. Peel the bananas and place in a bowl. Mash them with a fork until they're mushy.

8. Add the flour mixture, mashed bananas, and milk to butter mixture. Blend until all the dry ingredients are moistened (don't worry; it's supposed to be lumpy).

9. Stir in chocolate chips.

10. Make topping by mixing together the sugar and cinnamon in a small bowl.

11. Spoon the batter into the muffin cups, filling cups until they're almost full. Sprinkle topping onto each muffin.

12. Bake for 25 to 30 minutes. Check for doneness by inserting a toothpick in the center of a muffin; it will come out dry if the muffins are done.

13. Let the pan cool on a rack before removing the muffins. Store in an airtight container.

A Taste of the World

By Christine Venzon

Alton peered out the living room window to see who was ringing the bell. "Mom!" he called. "There's a strange girl at the door."

"We just moved here," his mom pointed out, stepping over cardboard boxes. "Everyone's a stranger."

"No, I mean she *looks* strange," Alton said.

"Not strange," his mother corrected, opening the door. "Just . . . colorful."

"Hello!" the girl said. "I'm Pam Deville. My family lives across the street. We wanted to welcome you to the neighborhood." She handed Alton's mom a plate piled with long, thin cookies drizzled with dark chocolate.

"Why, thank you," Alton's mom said. "Please come in."

Pam stepped inside. Alton got a better look at his new neighbor. She looked a little older than Alton, and she had on a long dress with stripes of black, mustard yellow, and lime green that zigzagged like stair steps. A string of fat beads and seashells hung from her neck. He also eyed the plate of cookies.

"I'll take those for you, Mom," he offered.

His mom held the plate tightly until she caught Alton's eye. "We'll save those for dessert tonight," she said emphatically.

Pam grinned as Alton's face fell. She said, "Actually, Mom would be happy if you tried one now. She's the food writer for the local newspaper. She thinks trying new food and sharing it with neighbors is one of the most fun things in life."

Alton looked at his mom hopefully. She smiled. "Sure, go ahead and have one."

Alton lifted the plastic wrap and took the biggest cookie. It was a surprise—crunchy and tasting of cherries and nuts as well as chocolate. A delicious surprise, he quickly decided. "They're like sweet, toasty slabs," he said.

"They *are* toasted," Pam explained. "They're Italian cookies called biscotti. That means 'twice cooked.' After you bake them, you slice them and toast them in the oven."

"Do you like cooking too, Pam?" his mom asked.

"I sure do. I'm kind of Mom's assistant. I really like finding recipes from different countries for her column. We got the idea to develop this one from an Italian Web site."

Alton munched with gusto. "If all your mom's recipes are like this, we'd better start getting that newspaper!"

A few days later, the biscotti were gone. Alton walked across the street to return the empty plate.

Pam greeted him at the door, dressed this time in jeans and a sweatshirt. "Alton, I'm glad you're here. Mom and I made one of our favorite recipes last night. When I told her how much you liked the biscotti, she made an extra batch for your family. Come in for a second and I'll get it for you."

Another tasty surprise, Alton thought. "Sure! And tell your mom thanks."

Pam disappeared into the kitchen. Gazing around the living room, Alton nearly jumped at the sight of a long wooden carving hanging on the wall. It looked like a person's face, but the deep brown cheeks had bands of gold speckles. It seemed to be wearing a tall, dark red headdress. The eyebrows stuck out with tufts of stiff hair.

Pam reappeared and handed him covered bowl. "It's African Chicken-Peanut Butter Stew," she announced.

Alton looked at the container suspiciously. Had he heard right? "I love peanut butter—but in stew? Can you do that?"

Pam laughed. "Sure you can. Chicken, peanut butter, onions, sweet potatoes, garlic— it's all in there."

"Um . . . well, I like my peanut butter with jelly."

"They probably do in Africa too," Pam said. "And also with fried fish, and greens, and rice. People in Africa were growing peanuts before the United States existed. They call them 'groundnuts.'"

Alton thought of the carving. "Is that thing on the wall from Africa, too?"

"It sure is." Pam sounded proud as she took the carving down from the wall. "From East Africa. A country called Kenya. The Masai people carve masks from native trees to honor their ancestors. This one's just for decoration."

Alton thought it looked even more bizarre up close. "It doesn't look like anything I'd put in my room," he declared.

"That's what I used to say," Pam said. "But think about it—do you have family pictures in your room?"

"Sure," he said. "Doesn't everyone?"

Pam smiled. "Not the Masai. They carve masks, like we take pictures. They use their skills and the materials on hand to remember the people they love."

Alton shrugged. "I guess it makes sense when you put it that way. How do you know so much about Africa, Pam?"

Pam carefully returned the carving to the wall. "My mom has a friend who moved to Kenya to go to school. She sent us this. They keep in touch by e-mail. Of course, Mom asks mostly about the food. But her friend makes it sound so fascinating, I started doing my own research on the Internet. Maybe I'll visit Kenya someday."

"Did she send those clothes you had on the other day?" Alton asked.

"No, but they *are* from Africa. I got them online from a clothing importer. The dress is made from kente cloth. That's from Ghana. They weave different patterns and colors to represent different qualities. The pattern I wore reminds people to forgive and be tolerant. I have another one that stands for trusting in God."

"Cool," Alton said. "It's like the T-shirts with slogans from my church's youth group."

"That's right," Pam agreed. "It's funny, isn't it? People around the world are different in so many ways. But if you look closer, we're all more alike than we think."

Alton thought about Pam's words on his walk back home. Meanwhile, the mouth-watering aroma of peanut butter rose to his nose. He opened the bowl as soon as he got to the kitchen.

His dad was hanging curtain rods over the kitchen window. "What do you have there, Alton?" he asked.

"Pam's mom made this," Alton said. "It's . . . um . . . chicken stew.

His dad looked into the bowl. "Smells good. What's in it?"

"Chicken and onions and sweet potatoes and . . . um, peanut butter too. I know that's weird and all," Alton admitted quickly, "but Pam said people in Africa love it, and, well, it can't be too bad if it's that popular, right? So . . . can we try it?"

"Sure," his dad said. "We can have it tonight, in fact. Call Mom and tell her not to pick up anything on her way home from work. We'll call Mrs. Deville and thank her later."

"Great! You're the coolest, Dad!" Alton reached for the cell phone—and a spoon. No one would miss one little bite . . .

African Chicken–Peanut Butter Stew

Peanuts are an important food in many different African cuisines. They're not truly nuts, but legumes, and they actually do grow underground. They're high in protein and add distinctive flavor in any recipe.

Remember to check with your parents before you make this stew. Some kids are allergic to peanuts!

Makes 4 servings

- 1 tablespoon olive oil
- 2 boneless, skinless chicken breasts halves, cut into 1/2-inch-wide strips
- 1 small yellow onion, chopped
- 2 medium cloves garlic, peeled and chopped
- 1 medium sweet potato, peeled and cut into 1-inch cubes
- 1 teaspoon ground cumin (you'll find cumin and ground coriander seed in the spice section at your grocery store)
- 1 teaspoon ground coriander seed

1/2 teaspoon dried red pepper flakes (optional)

1 can low-sodium chicken broth (14.5 ounces)

1 can garbanzo beans (chickpeas) with their liquid (15.5 ounces)

1/2 cup peanut butter, smooth or crunchy

1. In a large skillet, heat the oil over medium high heat. Add the chicken and cook, stirring, until browned.

2. Using a slotted spoon, take the chicken out of the pan and put it in a bowl.

3. Turn the heat to medium low. Add garlic, onion, and sweet potato to the pan, and cook for about 5 minutes.

4. Add the cumin, coriander seed, and red pepper flakes.

5. Mix in chicken broth and chicken.

6. Cover the skillet tightly and simmer on low, stirring once or twice, for about 15 minutes.

7. Add the garbanzo beans and the peanut butter, stirring to blend well.

8. Put the lid back on. Turn heat to medium. Once the stew begins to simmer again, stir and cook on low for about 2 minutes. Serve over white or brown rice, with a green salad on the side.

Am I Skinny Yet?

By Diana R. Jenkins

I pushed my tray down the lunch line, moving past the cheeseburgers and fries. Sadly, I stopped at the salad bar, where I plopped a few leaves of lettuce and a slice of tomato on a plate.

"Come on, Bob! Don't tell me you're on a diet again!"

I looked at Wade and his full lunch tray. "I have to lose weight."

Wade rolled his eyes. He's a good friend,

but he doesn't understand what it's like to be overweight.

We paid for our lunches and found seats in the cafeteria. My lunch was gone in a few bites! My stomach still felt as empty leaving the cafeteria as it had going in.

During social studies, my poor, hollow stomach growled so loudly that Mr. Diaz stopped talking about the War of 1812. "What was that?" he asked.

Seth shouted, "That's Bob's stomach!" It was so embarrassing when everyone laughed!

After class, Seth came up to me in the hall. "Some of us are trying to hear what the teacher's saying, so how about keeping the noise down?" His friends hee-hawed behind him, and Seth added, "See you later, Bob the Blob!"

After they walked away, I turned to Wade. "That's why I have to lose weight. I'm tired of people teasing me."

"But your crazy diets don't work!"

"Because I don't stick to them," I said. "But this time will be different."

After PE, I didn't buy my usual candy bar. I also skipped buying a soda for the bus ride home. When I got to my house, I went upstairs and got busy on my homework without a snack. Nothing was going to keep me from being skinny!

By suppertime, I was starving. After I ate three servings of everything, Mom said, "Goodness, Bob! I didn't know you liked this casserole so much!"

"It's really good, Mom," I said, even though I'm not a big fan of tuna.

That night I lay in bed feeling mad at myself. How could I lose weight eating like that?

The next morning, I had dry toast for breakfast. When I got to school, I smelled sweet rolls baking in the cafeteria, but I walked straight to my locker. All morning I resisted getting a snack.

By lunch time, I felt weak, but I sat down without getting a tray. It was spaghetti day, so the cafeteria smelled of tomato sauce and garlic bread. I was ready to give up and buy lunch when I heard Seth's voice behind me. "Look, guys, a beached whale!"

I pretended not to hear. They'll be so shocked when I lose weight, I thought. I'm going to be like a stick!

"There you are!" Wade slid into the seat across from me. "Aren't you eating anything?"

My mouth watered at the sight of Wade's spaghetti lunch, but I said, "No, I'm sticking to my diet."

"But, Bob," said Wade, "it's not healthy to starve yourself!"

"Whatever," I said.

In PE, I was so tired I could hardly dribble the basketball.

In English, I fell asleep.

When the dismissal bell rang at the end of math, I stood up and got this major head rush. For a minute there, I thought I was going to pass out!

"Are you okay?" asked Wade, grabbing my arm.

I shook off his hand. "I'm fine."

I wasn't, of course. I wasn't fine. I wasn't skinny. And I wasn't going to be able to stick to my diet for one more minute!

I got a soda and some candy for the bus ride. Then when I got home, I ate half a bag of cookies and drank more soda! At supper, I ate like a starving person. The next morning I wolfed down a huge breakfast. Then when I got to school, I bought two sweet rolls and sat down in the cafeteria to eat them.

Wade came along and plopped down beside me. "Look at this book I borrowed from my dad."

I glanced at the title: *Weight Loss the Healthy Way*. "I don't need that now. I gave up on my diet. Like always!" I took a BIG bite of sweet roll.

"Just look at it." He opened the book and pointed. "Here's a chapter about how to eat healthy and lose weight without starving yourself." He flipped through the pages and pointed again. "This part tells about exercise that's fun and not too hard—like walking. And this chapter—"

"—I hade ejertise," I said with my mouth full.

"I'll help you," said Wade. "We can do stuff together."

"Look, I know you're trying to be a friend, but let it go, okay?" I said. "I have never been able to stick to any kind of diet!"

"But this is about living healthy all the time—not dieting. Just try it!"

My heart felt heavy in my chest. "I don't think I can stand to start all over again," I said quietly.

Wade closed the book. "You know, you don't have to do it all alone."

"It's great that you want to help," I said.

"That's not what I meant," said Wade. "There's someone else you could ask to help you." He pointed upward and smiled.

I knew what he was saying, but since the office is right over the cafeteria, I said, "The principal?"

"Ha. Funny." Wade frowned at me. "I'm serious here, Bob."

I picked up the book and flipped through it myself. It did look like it had a lot of good information. And everything was more fun with Wade, so maybe I could manage some exercise if we did it together.

I closed the book and looked at the cover, but I didn't see it. I was thinking about Wade's idea of asking God for help. Quickly, I said a little prayer: *Please, Lord, help me make a fresh start. Help me find the strength to do what my body needs.*

I felt a little glimmer of hope growing in my heart then. Pushing the sweet rolls away, I said, "Okay, I'll try it."

"Great!" said Wade.

So I've followed the book's plan for three weeks. It hasn't been easy cutting out the sodas, sweets, and junk food that I love, but I haven't been hungry, either. I eat plenty of fruits and vegetables! And, believe it or not, whole-grain bread actually tastes good, once you get used to it.

Even with Wade along, exercise isn't always that fun. But I've already lost a good amount of weight, and I have more energy than I used to.

When things get tough, I pray, and that really helps me keep going. I've found that prayer helps me deal with the teasing, too. I'm glad that God is part of my new, healthy lifestyle!

Whole-Grain English Muffin Bread

Much to his surprise, Bob discovered that whole-grain breads are delicious! He likes to bake a loaf of this English muffin bread once a week or so—it makes great sandwiches, and it's really good toasted and spread with low-sugar jam.

This recipe will take about 2 to 3 hours in all, because you have to allow time for the dough to rise.

Makes one loaf

1 (.25 ounce) package active dry yeast

Butter or margarine for greasing bowl

1-1/4 cups warm water (it should be just warm enough to feel comfortable when you dip your wrist into it. Water that's steaming hot will kill yeast!)

1/3 cup whole-wheat flour

1/3 cup quick-cooking oats

1 tablespoon sugar

3/4 teaspoon salt

2-1/2 cups all-purpose flour, plus extra for sprinkling

1/4 cup cornmeal

1. In a large mixing bowl, dissolve the yeast in the warm water. Stir it gently for about 30 seconds. Butter a medium-size bowl.

2. In another medium bowl, mix together the whole-wheat flour, oats, sugar, salt, and 1-1/2 cups of the all-purpose flour (save the rest).

3. Add these dry ingredients to the water and yeast. Beat by hand (with a wooden spoon), or with an electric beater until smooth.

4. Beat in the remaining cup of all-purpose flour to make a soft dough. (Rub some flour on your hands, then use them to mix the dough as it gets thicker.)

5. Sprinkle flour on a clean countertop. Rub more flour on your hands, pick up the dough, and move it onto the floury surface. Use your hands to form the dough into a ball. Place it in the buttered bowl, turning the dough once so the top gets buttery.

6. Cover with a damp dish towel and let the dough rise in a warm place for about 1 hour, or until it's about

twice as large as it started out being. (You can let it rise for up to an hour longer if you need to.)

7. Once it's risen, wash and dry your hands. Then rub a little flour on one fist, and gently push it into the dough. (Don't worry—it's *supposed* to deflate!)

8. Now move the dough out of the bowl onto a surface that's been lightly sprinkled with flour. Turning the dough several times, shape it into a loaf.

9. Coat a 9 x 5 x 3-inch loaf pan with nonstick cooking spray. Sprinkle about half of the cornmeal onto the bottom and around the sides.

10. Place the loaf in the pan; sprinkle with the remaining cornmeal.

11. Cover the loaf with the damp dish towel and let rise again until doubled, about 1/2 hour to 1 hour.

12. While it's rising, preheat the oven to 400° F.

13. Bake the loaf for 30 minutes, or until it's golden brown. Tip: To check for doneness, tip it out of the pan (using an oven mitt, of course) and tap the bottom of the loaf. If it sounds hollow, it's done!

14. Cool the loaf completely on a wire rack before slicing. Store in a plastic bag.

Strawberry-Banana Smoothies

Eating more fruit is an important part of Bob's new, healthy lifestyle. This recipe makes 2 servings—so you can share with a friend! For 4 servings, just double the amounts.

You can use fresh berries instead of frozen, but remember to wash them and to cut off any green stems and leaves first.

1 banana, cut into pieces

3/4 cup frozen unsweetened strawberries (you can substitute frozen raspberries or blueberries for the strawberries)

1 container vanilla low-fat yogurt (8 ounces)

3/4 cup low-fat milk

1. In a blender, combine bananas, frozen strawberries, yogurt, and milk.

2. Put on the blender lid and whirr until smooth.

3. Pour into glasses and serve.

Grading Gran

By Donna R. Gamache

"I'm so glad you've come, Austin," my grandmother said when she met me at the airport. "I hope you'll enjoy your visit!"

I hoped so, too. But three weeks with a grandmother I barely knew wasn't my idea of a super vacation.

"I really want to attend the conference in Nicarauga," my mom had said, "and Grandmother Raynor has asked you to visit."

I couldn't say no. Gran Raynor is my dad's mom, but I hardly know her. That's because

Dad died eight years ago, when I was four, and because she lives three states away. We write and telephone, but I hadn't seen her for years. I wasn't even sure I'd recognize her!

As grandmothers go, she's not old, but I was sort of expecting a gray-haired lady in a dress. Instead she was wearing jeans, and her hair was bright reddish-brown. That was only the first of many surprises.

"I've planned all sorts of activities," Gran said as we left the airport. She started listing them—fishing, golf, horseback riding, to name a few—not grandmother-type activities, but twelve-year-old kid things! "We'll try fishing first," she added. "Your grandpa used to fish. His rod and tackle are still around."

I'd never tried fishing, but the very first morning she insisted on getting up at five o'clock and digging up worms from the back yard. We spent the whole day in a rented rowboat—casting, waiting for a nibble, casting again—all without a single bite.

"I guess I fail the fishing test," Gran joked afterward. "A big fat F."

"You're okay with the worms!" I told her.

She laughed and began planning the next activity—golf. That didn't work out any better. I'd never golfed before and if Gran had, her game didn't show it. After losing about six balls, we finally called it quits. Using Gran's grading system, it rated about a D!

"The next activity will be better, Austin," she assured me. "There's a cross-country ski trail where they ride bicycles in summer."

Two days later she borrowed bikes and a carrier. Only, they were just regular ten-speeds, no good on grassy ski-trails. Besides, I'll bet it was ten years since Gran rode a bike!

"Another F," I thought, as we pushed our bikes back up the hills. But I didn't say it out loud!

"You don't have to try all these activities for me," I told her, and for the next few days we stuck to easier things—a movie, a shopping trip, and a swim at the local pool. I rated them all a solid B.

Then she hit on a new idea—camping! "I've

found your grandpa's old tent in the garage," she said excitedly.

"I've never camped before," I told her. "Have you?"

"Sure. Not lately, but your grandpa and I used to camp when we were younger. We'll try a National Forestry campground in the foothills."

"What about bears? Or mountain lions?"

"They're usually scared of people. You just have to lock your food in the car."

She began to round up sleeping bags, mattresses, and food. I was still doubtful, but I didn't want Gran to think I didn't appreciate her efforts. Besides, I had orders from Mom: "Remember, Gran is going out of her way for you, so do what she asks." I just wondered if Mom had any idea what that meant!

By two o'clock the next day we'd found the campground, an open meadow surrounded by hills. We were the only campers there.

Gran dumped poles and pegs on the ground, then frowned. "Guess I forgot an axe or hammer to pound these in."

About then I wanted to give her a D, but instead I hunted out a strong branch to pound with; that didn't work. "Try your hiking boot," I suggested, and that did the trick, but it was a slow operation. By then I was starving. Fortunately, Gran had brought homemade cookies. Her grade went up!

"Time to blow up the air mattresses, "she announced. That was a long job, too. Then she asked me to gather wood for a fire.

"Get plenty of dry twigs and bark," she said, "since we can't cut kindling."

"You did remember matches?" I asked, and she held out a waterproof container. Luckily it hadn't rained, so everything was dry.

Then Gran showed me how to make a campfire. "For making chili later on," she said.

The campfire and chili were great. There were marshmallows, too, and toasted over the fire, they were the best! Even though they did go along with Gran's campfire singing, I was ready to give her an A+! "This was your best idea yet," I told her.

A few hours later I changed my mind. I woke to the sound of heavy rain on the tent and raindrops on my face. Gran switched on the flashlight to show three steady drips above me. "This tent has seen better days," she said. "Move your sleeping bag." Then she dashed out for containers to catch the drips.

There was enough room to rearrange things, but my sleeping bag was wet. That, and the rain pounding on the tent, and the sound of drips landing in the pail and pans kept me awake all night.

About when it started to get light, the rain eased off, but everything outside was soaking, including the firewood. "Oh, dear!" said Gran. "I brought bacon and eggs for a real camping breakfast, but I should've brought a camp stove." We settled for bread and peanut butter, and ate it in the tent. By the time we'd finished, the clouds were breaking up.

We emptied out the containers we'd used to catch water, wiped the picnic table dry, and draped my sleeping bag and some wood over it to dry out.

"Let's try a hike," Gran suggested, and, using a map, we headed upstream along a small creek. Except that my feet were soon soaked, it was a great day! Gran pointed out a hawk's nest, and raccoon and deer tracks. We snacked on more cookies, careful to follow the creek so we wouldn't get lost.

It was after three o'clock when we returned. Right away we saw our tent collapsed in a heap, alongside my sleeping bag on the grass.

"Uh-oh," said Gran, and pointed out large tracks as well as rips in the tent that looked like claw marks. "Looks like we've had a bear. We shouldn't have eaten breakfast in the tent. He probably smelled the peanut butter. Don't worry," she added. "I'm sure he's long gone now."

"But our tent!"

Gran sighed. "It's wrecked. I guess we'll have to pack up and head home."

We started loading. "This trip was a definite F. Or worse!" Gran said.

"I don't know, Gran. Some of it was fun. And

I sure learned a lot about camping. What to do—and what not to do," I added with a grin.

"You mean that, Austin?" Gran asked as she started up the car. "Good. Because I've got lots more ideas. I think we'll try horseback riding next!"

A+ Campfire-Style Chili

Even if you're not camping out like Gran and Austin, you'll enjoy making this hearty chili at home! It's great served with a green salad and Austin's favorite cornbread.

Serves 6 (leftovers can easily be reheated in the microwave)

   2 cans kidney or pinto beans (15.5 ounces each)

   1 pound lean ground beef

   1 cup diced onion (about 1 medium)

   2 cloves garlic, peeled and chopped

   1 can diced tomatoes in their liquid (28 ounces)

   1 can diced green chili peppers (4 ounces) (if you're not a fan of spicy food, you can leave these out)

   1/2 cup beef broth

   2 teaspoons chili powder

   1/2 teaspoon ground cumin (you'll find this in the spice section at your grocery store)

   1/2 cup shredded cheddar or Monterey Jack cheese

1. Open the cans of beans, drain them in a colander, and rinse them with water. Then pour the beans into a medium-size bowl.

2. On the stovetop, cook the ground beef, onion, and garlic over medium-high heat in a large deep-sided frying pan. Keep cooking and stirring until the beef is browned.

3. Using a slotted spoon, transfer the beef, onions, and garlic to the bowl with the beans, leaving the fat in the pan. Let it cool for a few minutes (sizzling fat is even hotter than boiling water!).

4. Set one of the empty bean cans in the sink and carefully pour the fat into it. (Later, after the fat fully cools and hardens, you can safely discard the can.)

5. Add the beans and the meat mixture back into the frying pan. Then add the tomatoes, chili peppers, beef broth, chili powder, and cumin. Bring to a boil. Stir, cover, and reduce heat to low.

6. Simmer, stirring frequently, for 20 to 25 minutes.

7. Ladle into bowls, sprinkle with cheese, and serve.

Austin's Favorite Cornbread

Makes 16 pieces

> 1-1/4 cups all-purpose flour
>
> 3/4 cup yellow or white cornmeal
>
> 1/4 cup sugar
>
> 2 teaspoons baking powder
>
> 1/2 teaspoon salt
>
> 1 cup milk
>
> 1/4 cup vegetable oil
>
> 1 egg, beaten slightly with a fork

1. Preheat oven to 400° F.

2. Grease an 8-inch-square pan.

3. Combine the flour, cornmeal, sugar, baking powder, and salt in a medium-size bowl and mix well.

4. Beat the milk, oil, and egg together in a small bowl. Add to the dry ingredients and stir until the dry ingredients are moistened (the batter is supposed to be a little lumpy).

5. Spread batter evenly in the baking pan.

6. Bake 20 to 25 minutes, until golden brown. (It's okay if the cornbread cracks on top.) When it's done, a toothpick inserted into the center will come out dry.

7. Let cool on a rack before cutting into squares. Store in an airtight container.

Unplugged for a Week

By Christine Brauer Mueller

Monday

Ted watched his best friend climb over the windowsill. Jimmy's lifeline to all things musical was stuck in his jeans pocket, and the earbuds dangled from the neck of his T-shirt. Flipping the bill of his baseball hat around, he surveyed the room.

"Gee, Ted! It's like a tomb in here!"

Ted propped himself up on one elbow. "I told you what they said—one whole week—no electricity in here, except for my lamp. I can't believe my parents flipped out like this just because I violated my curfew. I wasn't getting into trouble—we were just playing video games and I lost track of the time."

Jimmy laughed. "I think this is your fourth curfew violation, buddy!" He plopped down on the floor. "Can I keep you company?"

"Like you'd want to spend a whole week with me anyway. There's nothing to do."

Jimmy snorted. "You're acting like a spoiled brat. We can do lots of things. The weather is perfect for our bikes and blades."

Ted perked up at the thought of getting out of the house and escaping the sight of all his now-useless technological toys.

Two hours later, he parked his bike in the garage and joined his family for dinner. His mother passed him a second helping of lasagna.

"You certainly are hungry tonight," his father said.

Ted forgot he was going to stay mad at him. "Yeah, we took the eight-mile trail through the park, and Jimmy kept up with me the whole way. He's really in shape after running track this year." Ted caught his brother smirking. "What? You think I'm not in good shape?"

His brother chuckled. "I don't know. Which finger operates the remote? That one's probably in pretty good shape."

Ted's sister chimed in, "Or maybe his wrists, operating the joystick for all those computer games he plays."

His brother and sister were so annoying! Ted asked to be excused. He could hear the two of them laughing as he went up to his room. Man, it really *was* as dark as a tomb in there!

He yanked back the curtains and flicked up the window shade. It flipped noisily over its roller. The room looked better lit by the setting sun. He waved to Jimmy mowing his front yard across the street.

The Reds and the Indians were playing tonight, but he couldn't watch or listen to the game. He'd have to read the scores in the paper in the morning. He couldn't check his e-mail, he couldn't burn any CDs, he couldn't surf the Net looking for guitar tabs, and he couldn't even call his friends. The thought of six more days without technology was depressing. Ted went to bed early.

Tuesday

"Great! It's raining," Ted muttered as he crawled over the side of his bunk. He could see the blank TV screen and the computer monitor staring back at him like two blind eyeballs. He slammed the bedroom door in disgust and thumped down the stairs to fix breakfast.

"So what's happening today, Mr. Sunshine?" his sister asked.

"Probably best to leave Ted alone, honey. He doesn't seem to be in a very good mood this morning."

Ted glared at his mother, but decided to keep quiet. No point in getting any more techno-free days added to his punishment.

He showered and then took two extra towels from the linen closet and hung them over the TV and the computer so he wouldn't have to look at them.

After school he sorted his old baseball card collection and felt sorry for himself.

Wednesday

Bored after school, Ted tried to take a nap, but his mother woke him by running the vacuum cleaner.

"Hey, no electricity in here, Mom!"

"Not for you, dear. I can use all I want. In your case, though, I'd be glad to make an exception for cleaning. Just say the word!"

Ted stalked out of the room and down to the kitchen. His stomach growled. He yelled up the stairs, "Hey, Mom! Do you care if I make muffins?"

Getting the okay, he pulled out the eggs, milk, and packaged mix.

The smell of nearly-done blueberry muffins brought his sister to the kitchen. "You planning on eating all of them, Ted, or can I have one?"

Ted's brother just grabbed a couple and ran out on the porch to wolf them down. Ted poured a glass of milk and ate four at a leisurely pace. He wrapped two for each of his parents and warned his brother and sister to not to eat them.

Still bored, he decided to bake pre-packaged cookies from a roll to kill time. He took a plate over to Jimmy's house after dinner.

"They're pretty good, but next time, bake that special kind your mom makes," Jimmy said between munches. "The triple chocolate ones."

"Yeah—I bet I could learn to make those."

Thursday

Getting off the bus, Jimmy reminded Ted, "Don't forget! You promised to help me clean the garage!"

Later, as they were finishing up, Jimmy said, "I like this punishment of yours, Ted. I've never had you offer to help with a job like this before."

"You probably won't ever again either!" Ted laughed as he carried out old paint cans for the recycling center. At five o'clock Jimmy's father hauled the recyclables off. Ted and Jimmy split a Popsicle before he went home. Tomorrow was fall break—a three-day weekend.

Friday

That morning, Ted didn't even glance at his computer and TV shrouded in towels. The sun was out and the air was crisp when he walked the dog. He and Jimmy decided to take Jimmy's little sister rollerblading at the park. He wanted them to try out the path he'd discovered to the new levee walk.

His mother was in a wonderful mood. Probably from all those cookies, he thought. She even made real mashed potatoes to go with the pork roast for dinner.

Saturday

Ted invited Jimmy over to help clean out his room. *Jim owes me after that garage job*, he thought, as he picked at the grime under his fingernails.

Jimmy helped carry the TV to the playroom

in the basement. "Aren't you going to miss it up here?"

"I don't think so. Don't worry—I'm not becoming a technophobe. The computer and stereo stay."

"So I'll still see that warm glow of the computer screen outlining your shades!" Jimmy laughed.

"Only at night. I'm starting to like the look of daylight in here," Ted replied.

Sunday

Ted's father gave him a high-five after church. "So, son, did you thank God that this week's finally over?"

Ted nodded. "Yeah. But you know what? I think I learned how to get along without all my techno-toys."

"Anything else?"

"Oh—yeah. I should get home on time so you and Mom don't have to worry about me. And if I'm going to be late I should call. Maybe you could get me a cell phone for my birthday?"

Ted's mother rolled her eyes. "So much for learning to live without technology! How about if I teach you to bake those cookies from scratch instead?"

Ted grinned. "How about a double batch?"

Triple Chocolate Cookies

Ted taught his friend Jimmy to make these great cookies, too.

Makes about 2 dozen

1/2 cup (1 stick) butter, softened

3/4 cup packed dark brown sugar (to measure, tamp it down with a spoon)

1 egg

1 teaspoon vanilla extract

1 cup all-purpose flour

1/2 cup unsweetened cocoa powder

1/2 teaspoon baking soda

1/8 teaspoon salt

1/2 cup semisweet chocolate chips

1/2 cup white chocolate chips

1. Preheat oven to 350° F.

2. In a large bowl, beat together the butter, sugar, egg, and vanilla until fluffy. (You can use an electric beater, or beat by hand with a wooden spoon.)

3. Combine the flour, cocoa, baking soda, and salt in a medium-size bowl.

4. Add the dry ingredients, about 1/4 cup at a time, to the butter mixture, beating well. (The batter will be stiff.)

5. Stir in all the chocolate chips.

6. Drop by rounded teaspoonfuls onto ungreased cookie sheets (allow room for the cookies to spread as they bake).

7. Bake for 8 to 10 minutes, or until the centers are set. (The cookies will be starting to crinkle on top.)

8. Cool for about 3 minutes on the cookie sheets, then, using a thin metal spatula, move the cookies to a wire rack to cool completely. Store in an airtight container.

Attack of the Cousins!

By Diana R. Jenkins

They came at night.

They came without warning.

I wish I could say they came in peace!

Oh, they were quiet enough at first, sleeping in their parents' arms as they walked in our front door. Uncle Bill and Aunt Kat had sent us pictures of their four-year-old twins, Bailey and Bryan, but the kids were even cuter in person.

"Put them in Ada's room," said Mom. "She'll love having her cousins stay with her, won't you, Ada?"

My parents are big on being nice to company so I said, "Sure!"

Dad set up air mattresses on my bedroom floor, and my aunt and uncle put the twins to bed. They looked like angels, I thought, as I turned out the light.

Early the next morning, an elephant jumped on me, yelling, "Ada! Ada!" I burrowed under the covers, but the elephant didn't go away, so I opened my eyes.

Bailey was sitting on my stomach, still yelling. Bryan stood nearby. "Are you mad?" he asked in a quivery voice.

Tears were welling up in his eyes. Obviously he was a sensitive little guy. "Hey, I like getting up early," I told him.

"Ada!" shrieked Bailey.

"What!" I yelled back.

She touched her nose to mine. "Are you awake?" she asked.

"I think so," I said. "Please get off me."

I went to the bathroom and got back just in time to see Bailey jump off my bed onto an air mattress. It let out a belch, then deflated with one long sigh.

"It broke!" wailed Bryan. Instant tears rolled down his checks.

"It's okay," I said. "You didn't break it." I gave Bailey the evil eye.

She shouted, "What's for breakfast?"

I told the kids to be quiet so our parents could sleep, but Bailey clomped down the hall like a one-girl herd of buffaloes. (She was wearing my hiking boots!) In the kitchen, she opened the refrigerator door so hard it bounced off the wall.

Bryan jumped, then looked at me, his bottom lip quivering.

"Don't worry," I told him. Then I turned and saw that Bailey had a bottle of grape soda in a bear hug. "You can't have that for breakfast!"

"Mommy lets us," said Bailey.

Aunt Kat isn't the most ordinary person on earth. "Is that true, Bryan?" I asked. He looked from me to Bailey to me, then burst into tears.

Bailey had a death grip on that soda, and I figured it wasn't polite to yank something away from a guest. "I know," I said, acting excited. "I'll make you guys some French toast!" And to make it sound more fun I added, "Shaped like stars!"

Bailey's eyes lit up, and even Bryan looked a little less pained.

"I want to help!" hollered Bailey.

"Me, too," said Bryan. "Please?"

"Okay," I said. "But let's put the soda back." Bailey and I wrestled over the bottle until she suddenly let go and I ended up sitting on the floor. She laughed her head off, but I didn't say anything, since Bryan was already whimpering.

As I got up, I prayed, *Please, Lord, give me patience!* "Okay!" I said cheerfully. "Let's fix the bread first."

Bailey was pretty good at shaping the bread with the star cookie cutter, but when she saw me get out the eggs, she decided they were more fun than bread. She tossed the cutter onto the floor. Bryan sobbed once.

"It's okay," I reassured him. After washing the cookie cutter, I let him finish cutting the bread stars while Bailey and I did the eggs. Bailey pulverized eggs instead of cracking them gently, so we went through half a carton just trying to get three into the bowl!

After I spooned all the bits of eggshell out of the glop and added the other ingredients, I gave each kid a turn at whisking the mixture. Some of it splashed onto the walls and counter, but there was enough left for dipping the bread. I did the cooking, since I was afraid to let the kids near the stove.

After all that work, I was happy that the kids loved the French toast. The quart or so of maple syrup Bailey grabbed and poured on helped, of course. While we ate, I hoped an adult would get up soon. Afterward, Bailey clomped to the bathroom, I cleaned up the kitchen, and Bryan followed me everywhere. I was afraid he'd cry if I told him to get out of my way.

When we went back to my room, Bailey was already there, wearing my underpants on her head.

"Take those off!" I cried, clapping my hands over Bryan's eyes.

She giggled, took off the panties, and threw them across the room. I gritted my teeth and prayed, *Help me, Lord!*

"Ouch!" cried Bryan. My hands were clamped too tightly over his little face.

"Sorry!" I said, letting go.

"What's the surprise?" he asked.

"What surprise?"

He whined, "Why did you hide my eyes?" His face was already crumpling.

"Uh . . . here!" I gave him the toy snake I won at the fair. He looked thrilled.

"What about me?" demanded Bailey. She was now wearing a black marker mustache.

"Well . . ."

"No fair!" she shouted.

"Give me a minute!" I said.

She folded her arms.

Desperately, I looked around for something to satisfy her. That's when I noticed that the white cat on the poster over my bed had a black mustache. In fact, every animal, person, and flower on every one of my posters was wearing a mustache!

"I'm waiting!" said Bailey.

Slowly I turned. "Why did you mess up my posters?" I demanded through clenched teeth.

She whipped a marker—my marker!—out of her pocket. "I decorated them. I'll give you a mustache, too!"

"No. You. Won't."

Bailey lowered her hand.

Bryan's lip began trembling.

"Don't even start," I told him.

He sucked his lip back in and sniffled just once.

"Sit down!" I ordered. To my surprise, the twins plopped right down on my bed.

"Now listen up!" I snapped. "You guys—"

They were looking up at me with BIG eyes.

I took a breath and said one more prayer for patience. "Listen," I said more nicely. "I'm glad you're here, but you have to behave. If you do, we'll have lots of fun. Okay?"

They nodded together.

"So . . . so give me my marker. No more markers unless I say so!" Bailey handed it over. I got down a game and started setting it up on the floor.

"I'm sorry," said Bailey.

"Me, too," said Bryan.

"It's okay," I said.

"How about some breakfast?" Dad came in with Aunt Kat behind him.

"Ada made us French toast already," said Bailey. "It was yummy!"

"But I was planning a big family breakfast," Dad complained.

"Oh, let them play," said Aunt Kat. "We have a whole week for family breakfasts."

"A week?" I squeaked.

"Yes!" grinned Dad. "A nice, long visit!"

Bailey looked up and smiled at me—just a friendly smile, I guess. It was probably the mustache that made her look like a little devil!

French Toast Stars

The twins loved Ada's star-shaped French toast!

Makes 4 servings

8 slices white or oatmeal bread

3 eggs

1/4 cup milk

1/4 teaspoon ground cinnamon

1/2 teaspoon vanilla extract

2 tablespoons butter

1. Lay out 4 slices of bread on a cutting board. Using a star-shaped cookie cutter, carefully cut out as many stars as possible (the final number will depend on how large your cutter is). You may have to pick up the bread and "pop" the star shape out from behind. Save the surrounding bread pieces with the star-shaped holes—you'll be cooking those, too!

2. Repeat for the last 4 slices of bread. Pile your bread stars and cut-out pieces onto a plate.

3. In a medium bowl, whisk together the eggs, milk, cinnamon, and vanilla extract.

4. In a frying pan, melt 1 tablespoon of the butter over medium heat. Tilt the pan to coat it with the butter.

5. Dip both sides of the stars in the egg mixture, then carefully place them into the hot butter.

6. After a minute or two, use a spatula to lift each star and check it. When they're golden brown, flip each one, then cook until golden on the second side. (When all the stars are cooked, you'll have to add the second tablespoon of butter to the pan before cooking the bread outlines.)

7. Put the French toast pieces on a plate and cover loosely with foil to keep them warm until they're all cooked.

8. Serve with maple syrup.

Stuffed French Toast

Note: If you're in the mood for something a bit fancier, try this variation. It works best with whole pieces of bread. In addition to the ingredients listed on page 105, you'll need:

4 ounces softened cream cheese

1/3 cup jam or preserves

Using a table knife, spread the cream cheese on four of the bread slices. Then spread the jam on the remaining four. Top each cream cheese slice with a jam slice, making four "sandwiches" with filling.

Now go back to following the French toast recipe on page 106, starting with step number 3.

The Breakfast Battle

By Leanne K. Currie-McGhee

Jack dashed into the kitchen, whizzing past his little sister, Carla.

"Jack Sprat, fast as a cat!" Carla teased.

"Ha, ha." Jack grabbed his backpack and rushed for the door.

"Where do you think you're going?" His mother placed her hands on her hips. "It's time for breakfast!"

Jack sighed and walked over to the kitchen table.

The breakfast battle had erupted when Jack started sixth grade. Every day Jack tried to race out of the house before breakfast. He wanted to meet his friends for doughnuts. Every day, his mother caught him and forced him to eat a healthy breakfast.

Jack made a face when he saw what his mother was stirring. "Oatmeal again. Yuck!"

"Sit, mister." His mom scooped gooey lumps into a bowl. She sprinkled brown sugar onto the oatmeal. "This will make it more palatable," she said.

"What's palatable?" asked Carla.

Jack swirled the oatmeal with his spoon. "Not this. What a boring breakfast."

His mother sipped her coffee as she studied the oatmeal. A small smile crossed her face. "Maybe it is a bit boring."

The next morning Jack swooped into the kitchen.

"Jack Sprat flies like a bat!" Carla greeted him.

Jack dashed to the door, but his mother stood in front of it with folded arms. "Breakfast, Bub."

Jack slunk into a wooden chair. "Oatmeal again?"

"No. I hope you know how to use these." His mom handed him a pair of red chopsticks.

"Chopsticks?" Jack wrinkled his forehead.

His mother carried a plate filled with little rice squares wrapped in what looked like black crinkly paper. Inside the middles of the squares were bits of pink, orange, and green.

Jack frowned. "What's this?"

"Today is Japanese morning. I thought you might enjoy a healthy breakfast if it was more exciting. It's a sushi roll made up of carrots, avocado, and cooked shrimp rolled in rice and wrapped with seaweed." His mom grinned.

"Seaweed!" Jack shrieked. "Gross!"

"Your sister likes it. And so do I."

After his mom said grace, Jack watched as she and his sister deftly used the chopsticks to pick up the rice squares.

Jack raised the sushi to his mouth. He nibbled it, prepared to spit it out. He blinked when he realized he actually liked the taste, but didn't let his mom know that. "I'll eat it so you don't bug me, Mom."

The following morning Jack jogged down the steps into the kitchen. He pretended to race as usual, but he stopped at the door. The kitchen smelled like spicy chicken soup.

"Jack Sprat, quick as a rat!" Carla exclaimed.

Jack turned to his mother.

"Thailand day!" she said. "The Thai people enjoy wonderful soups for breakfast." She inhaled. "Chicken with ginger. You'll love it!"

"Yeah, right." Jack dropped into a chair. Without being asked, he sipped the soup. It did taste good—delicious, actually— but he only muttered, "It's okay."

Over the next few days the family journeyed to India, Tonga, and France. One morning they had breakfast burritos and Mexican hot chocolate. It was awesome! Jack started looking forward to breakfast, but he didn't tell that to his mom. He didn't want her to think she'd "won" the breakfast battle.

On Sunday, Jack dressed for church. Then he jumped down the stairs and peeked into the kitchen. His mom sat reading a newspaper. Carla was eating . . . oatmeal.

Oatmeal? Jack raised his eyebrows. "What's today's country?"

His mother flipped a page. "Oh, Jack. I thought you didn't like the around-the-world breakfasts. You win. After today, you can eat doughnuts with your friends." She stood up. "I'm going to read the paper in the living room. We leave for Mass in an hour."

Jack felt Carla staring at him. "Don't say anything," he muttered. He hadn't meant to make his mom feel bad. Winning the breakfast battle didn't feel like winning at all.

Just then, his eyes fell on a world map held up by magnets on the refrigerator. He walked over and studied it. With a grin, he opened the refrigerator.

Fifteen minutes later, Jack's mom walked

back into the kitchen and stopped abruptly. Jack was carrying a loaded tray to the kitchen table.

"What are you up to, Jack?" his mom asked.

"Happy Greece Day, Mom! Last week I learned about Greece in school. I even learned what Greek people eat. So I made you breakfast." Jack handed his mom a plate.

She sat down and shook her head in disbelief. "You made me breakfast?"

"Yep. Pitas, feta cheese, and olives!" He paused and met his mom's eyes. "I really liked your world breakfasts, Mom. Thanks."

Jack's mom gave him her best smile. "Does this mean you'll make breakfast every day?" she teased.

Jack laughed. "How about we eat your breakfasts most of the time, and I meet my friends just once a week for unhealthy doughnuts?"

His mom munched on a pita and swallowed. "It's a deal! Just think—there are almost 200 countries left to try!"

"Jack Sprat will get fat," Carla said with a giggle. Jack playfully punched her arm and wondered where in the world they'd be eating breakfast tomorrow!

Breakfast Burritos

One country Jack really enjoyed "visiting" at breakfast was Mexico. Here are some versions of popular recipes based on Mexican food.

Serves 4

- 4 large flour tortillas

- 4 pieces bacon, cooked and crumbled

- 1 cup shredded sharp cheddar or Monterey Jack cheese

- 1/2 medium red bell pepper, chopped into small pieces

- 6 large eggs

- 1 tablespoon milk

- Dash salt

- 3 tablespoons chopped flat-leaf parsley

- 1 tablespoon butter

- Salsa—mild, medium, or hot (optional)

1. Preheat oven to 300° F.

2. Lay out the tortillas on a baking sheet.

3. Place cooked, crumbled bacon and shredded cheese down the center of each tortilla. Top with diced red bell pepper.

4. Combine eggs, milk, salt, and parsley in a small bowl or glass measuring cup. Whisk mixture with a fork until evenly combined.

5. Place the tortilla pan into the oven. (The heat will soften the tortillas and melt the cheese while you cook the eggs.)

6. In a frying pan, melt the butter over medium low heat. (Tip the pan so the butter coats the bottom.)

7. Add the egg mixture to the pan and let it sit for a minute or two, until the eggs just barely start to set.

8. Using a spatula, start moving the eggs from the outside of the pan toward the center. Keep gently scrambling them this way as they cook. When the eggs are soft and cooked through, take them off the heat.

9. Meanwhile, check the tortilla pan. When the cheese is melted, take the tortillas out of the oven and put each one on a plate.

10. Divide the eggs evenly among the tortillas, then carefully roll the tortillas into wraps. Top each burrito with a spoonful of salsa, if you like it.

Mexican Hot Chocolate

Serves 4

1/4 cup unsweetened cocoa powder

1/4 cup granulated sugar

3/4 teaspoon ground cinnamon

Dash of salt

Pinch of chili powder (optional—you can add another pinch if you like spiciness)

4 cups milk

1/4 cup half-and-half

3/4 teaspoon vanilla extract

1. In a small bowl, combine cocoa, sugar, cinnamon, chili powder (if you're using it), and salt.

2. Over medium-low heat, heat 1 cup of the milk in a saucepan until it's very hot but not boiling.

3. Take it off the heat and stir in the cocoa mixture, whisking until smooth.

4. Move the pan back onto the stove, stirring constantly. Stir in the remaining 3 cups of milk and heat again till very hot.

5. Whisk the mixture until it's frothy. Then stir in the half-and-half and vanilla.

6. Heat the mixture again, without boiling, until it's just the right temperature to drink.

Recipe Index

A+ Campfire-Style Chili	82
African Chicken-Peanut Butter Stew	60
Aunt Lil's Magic Muffins	49
Austin's Favorite Cornbread	84
Breakfast Burritos	115
Creative Chicken Salsa Soup	20
Frankie's Dipping Sauce	43
French Toast Stars	105
Grandpa's Dipping Sauce	43
Hermits (that Almost Crushed Cliveden)	31
Mexican Hot Chocolate	117
Mrs. Tran's Vietnamese Spring Rolls	41
Strawberry-Banana Smoothies	73
Stuffed French Toast	107
Triple Chocolate Cookies	95
Whole-Grain English Muffin Bread	70

Friend 2 Friend
Twelve Short Stories
Edited by Diane M. Lynch

Have you ever needed a friend, gotten mad at a friend, or been driven crazy by a friend? Have you ever felt as though you couldn't make it through life's tough spots without your friends? And have you ever wondered how you could be an even better friend yourself?

Well, so have the kids in this collection of twelve short stories. Enjoy meeting them as they experience the ups and downs of one of God's greatest gifts to us—the gift of friendship!

Paperback
112 pp.
26855
$7.95 U.S.

Stepping Stones
The Comic Collection
Written by Diana R. Jenkins
Art by Chris Sabatino

Denver, Chantal, Suki, and Alberto are on a journey—and
you can join them! With these fun and inspiring comics,
you'll share the ups and downs, problems and joys,
successes and failures of a great group of friends. The
stepping stones of their lives are leading them on a path
toward God.

Won't you follow along? After all, you're on that journey,
too!

Paperback
128 pp.
71184
$9.95 U.S.

Saints of Note
The Comic Collection
Written by Diana R. Jenkins
Art by Patricia Storms

Join time-travelers Paul and Cecilia as they journey to the past, meet saints, and become inspired to be better people. Their exciting adventures bring the saints to life and make them meaningful for today.

In addition to the comics, you'll also find detailed biographies, fascinating facts, interesting quotes, and other useful material to teach you even more about the saints. You'll enjoy *Saints of Note*, learn a lot—and get inspired, too!

Paperback
96 pp.
71206
$8.95 U.S.

Between You & Me, God

Prayers by Catholic Kids
Edited by Diane M. Lynch

In this prayer collection, kids from all over the United States and Canada open their hearts to God—and let him know what's on their minds.

They write about eating disorders, keeping up with schoolwork, dealing with stress, and celebrating the joys (and challenges) of daily life. They share hopes and fears about the problems in our world, and call on their favorite saints for support. A section of favorite Catholic prayers is also included.

We hope this prayer book will inspire you to open your heart to God, too!

Paperback
144 pp.
11718
$9.95 U.S.

Who are the Daughters of St. Paul?

We are Catholic sisters. Our mission is to be like Saint Paul and tell everyone about Jesus! There are so many ways for people to communicate with each other. We want to use all of them so everyone will know how much God loves us. We do this by printing books (you're holding one!), making radio shows, singing, helping people at our bookstores, using the Internet, and in many other ways.

Visit our Web site at www.pauline.org

BOOKS & MEDIA

The Daughters of St. Paul operate book and media centers at the following addresses. Visit, call or write the one nearest you today, or find us on the World Wide Web, www.pauline.org

CALIFORNIA
3908 Sepulveda Blvd, Culver City, CA 90230	310-397-8676
2640 Broadway Street, Redwood City, CA 94063	650-369-4230
5945 Balboa Avenue, San Diego, CA 92111	858-565-9181

FLORIDA
145 S.W. 107th Avenue, Miami, FL 33174	305-559-6715

HAWAII
1143 Bishop Street, Honolulu, HI 96813	808-521-2731
Neighbor Islands call:	866-521-2731

ILLINOIS
172 North Michigan Avenue, Chicago, IL 60601	312-346-4228

LOUISIANA
4403 Veterans Memorial Blvd, Metairie, LA 70006	504-887-7631

MASSACHUSETTS
885 Providence Hwy, Dedham, MA 02026	781-326-5385

MISSOURI
9804 Watson Road, St. Louis, MO 63126	314-965-3512

NEW JERSEY
561 U.S. Route 1, Wick Plaza, Edison, NJ 08817	732-572-1200

NEW YORK
64 W. 38th Street, New York, NY 10018	212-754-1110

PENNSYLVANIA
9171-A Roosevelt Blvd, Philadelphia, PA 19114	215-676-9494

SOUTH CAROLINA
243 King Street, Charleston, SC 29401	843-577-0175

VIRGINIA
1025 King Street, Alexandria, VA 22314	703-549-3806

CANADA
3022 Dufferin Street, Toronto, ON M6B 3T5	416-781-9131